Curlee Girlee

by
Atara
Twersky

illustrated by
Karen Wolcott

Publishers Cataloging-in-Publication Data

Twersky, Atara.
    Curlee Girlee / by Atara Twersky; illustrated by Karen Wolcott.
        p.cm.
    In English.
    Summary: Curlee Girlee's hair makes her mad! She wants it to grow down her back like spaghetti, not sideways and all curly-whirly. Curlee Girlee wants to look like everybody else—and she'll try anything to solve her problem. Then one day she discovers that her curly hair is perfect just the way it is. Curlee Girlee doesn't need to look like everyone else to be beautiful.
    ISBN-13: 978-0-9968438-1-2
    [1. General—Juvenile fiction. 2. Self-Esteem & Self-Reliance—Juvenile fiction. 3. Humorous Stories—Juvenile fiction.] I. Wolcott, Karen, ill. II. Title.

                                                                                            2016901746

To A and E, the best big sister and brother
any Curlee Girlee could ever have, and who
make every day an amazing adventure.

To *my* Curlee Girlee, whose beautiful hair
and matching personality inspired this book.

To my husband for his endless,
boundless love and encouragement.

And to Gab, who has loved Curlee Girlee from the beginning.

Production Date: October, 2018
Batch Number: 82897
Plant Location: GUANGDONG CHINA

Printed in China by Four Colour Print Group, Louisville, Kentucky
Fourth Edition

Design and text layout by margaretcogswell@gmail.com

When Curlee Girlee was a baby,
she wasn't Curlee Girlee. She didn't have
curly hair. She didn't have straight hair.
She didn't have any hair at all.

3

She loved to play with her big sister Emma and her big brother Alex. Most of the time, they loved to play with her, too.

4

As Curlee got older,
her arms and legs grew.
Her hands and feet grew.
Her tummy grew.
Even her fingers and toes grew.
But her hair refused to grow.

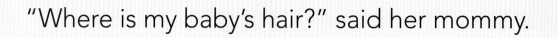

"Where is my baby's hair?" said her mommy.

"Where is baby sister's hair?" said Emma.

"Where is her hair?" whispered
the girl in the candy store.

Although she couldn't say it out loud,
or even put it into words, Curlee wished
hard for hair—lots of beautiful hair!

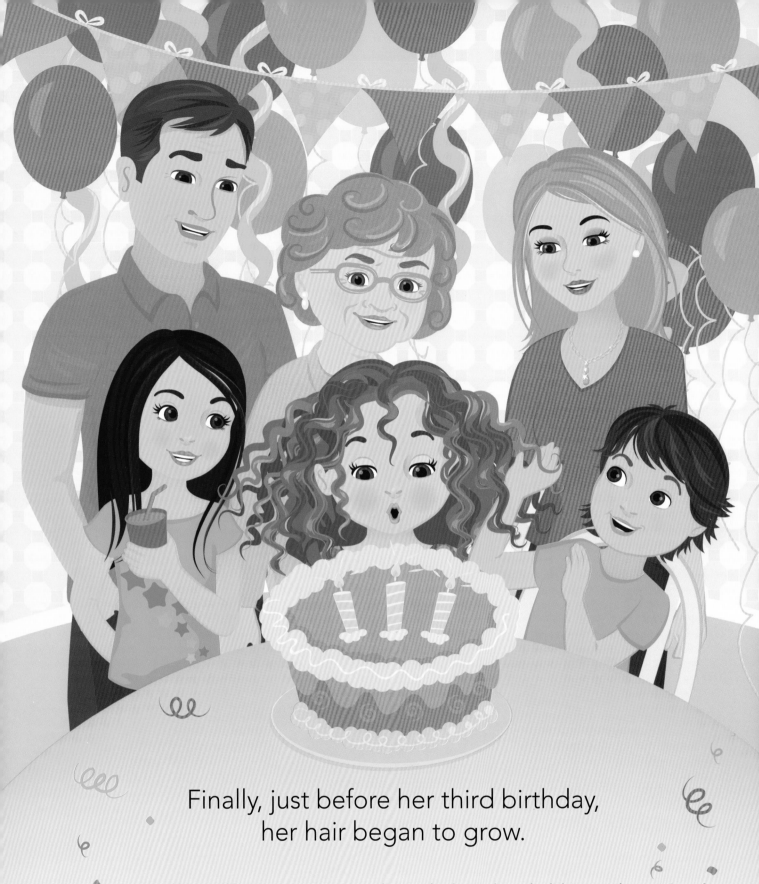

Finally, just before her third birthday,
her hair began to grow.

Well really, it *sprouted*. It didn't look like other
people's hair at all. Curlee's hair was swoopy
and loopy. It was bouncy and flouncy. When
she pulled it, it sprang right back!

That's when Mommy began to call her
"Curlee Girlee." Soon, everybody else did, too. Every
night at bedtime, Mommy asked, "Who is my
favorite Curlee Girlee in the world?"

Every morning at breakfast, Curlee Girlee looked at her sister's long, silky-milky hair. She looked at her brother's shiny, wavy-gravy bangs.

She decided she *really* wanted to look like everyone else.

When Curlee looked in the mirror, she stuck out her tongue.

She made sad puppy-dog-eye faces.

She pulled on her curls— but they popped right back.

Curlee Girlee wanted her hair to grow down her back like spaghetti.

She did not want it to grow sideways and make her look like a plant.

12

"Mommy, can you straighten my hair?" said Curlee Girlee when she saw her Mommy drying her own hair.

"Oh, no, Curlee Girlee," said Mommy. "You are beautiful just the way you are. Your hair makes you my special Curlee Girlee!"

13

Curlee Girlee got a brush and some water
and tried to straighten it herself.

At first it seemed straighter—but as it dried,
it got pouffier and fouffier and messier than ever.

Mommy uses a rolling pin when she makes blueberry pie. Maybe I can use it to uncurl my curls, thought Curlee Girlee.

She grabbed the rolling pin from the flour jar and rolled it over her curls. There was flour on the floor,
flour on the counter,
flour on her nose.
There was flour everywhere!

But Curlee Girlee still didn't have straight hair.

15

Maybe if I make special shampoo like Mommy uses,
I can fix my hair forever, thought Curlee Girlee.

She started pulling things off Mommy's shelves.
She mixed honey, cinnamon, and strawberry syrup.
This smells yummy, she thought, *and it is just
the right amount of goopy to work.*

But when she rubbed it on her head,
she was just a sticky, icky mess!

"MY HAIR MAKES ME SO MAD!" screamed Curlee Girlee—and Mommy came running.

She hugged Curlee Girlee tight and said, "Oh, sweetheart, someday you will love your curly-whirly hair. Now, let's wash this gloppy goo away!"

That night, Curlee Girlee dreamed that her hair grew longer and curlier than ever. It became a flying magic carpet. Up and away and into the clouds she flew with Alex and Emma.

On a cloud sat Grandma Maddie. She gave Curlee Girlee two magic barrettes and promised they would make her hair just the way she liked it. Curlee Girlee hid the barrettes under her pillow and promised Grandma she would wear them the next day.

The next morning, Curlee Girlee felt under
her pillow for the magic barrettes.
No barrettes.
She looked under the blanket.
No barrettes.
She grabbed her pillowcase and shook it hard,
but still there were no barrettes—only feathers
and feathers and more feathers!

Curlee Girlee ran into Emma's room. "Emma, did you take my magic barrettes?" she screamed as she jumped on Emma's bed.

"Can't you see I'm sleeping?" said Emma. "Go away!"

Maybe they are in Mommy's closet, thought
Curlee Girlee. She ran in there and began
pulling things off the shelves. Suddenly, a bunch
of boxes came tumbling down. Out of them
spilled lots and lots of very old pictures.

Curlee Girlee loved to look at pictures.

There was one of Curlee Girlee when she
was a baby with no hair at all…

One of Curlee Girlee and her sister splashing in the pool…

One of Mommy and Daddy all dressed up fancy-shmancy…

Then Curlee Girlee saw something amazing. It was a picture of a curly-haired girl who looked a lot like her!

But...she's beautiful! thought Curlee Girlee.

"Curlee Girlee, what are you doing in my closet?" said Mommy.

"Mommy! Who is this?" she said, holding up the old photo.

"It's your Grandma Maddie when she was young,"
said Mommy. "You got your fantastic hair from her."

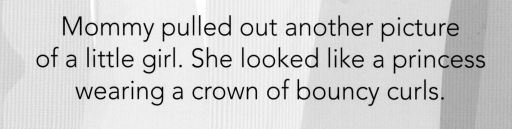

Mommy pulled out another picture
of a little girl. She looked like a princess
wearing a crown of bouncy curls.

"This is Grandma when she was just your age,"
said Mommy. "You see how pretty she was?
Just like Curlee Girlee!"

"Mommy, can I keep these pictures?"
asked Curlee Girlee.

"Of course you can," said Mommy.

That night, after Mommy tucked her into
bed and said goodnight, Curlee Girlee reached
under her pillow where she had put the pictures. She
looked at them and imagined herself growing up
with wild, curly, very special hair. She would look
just like Grandma Maddie—the most beautiful
person she had ever seen.

A year later—but in just the blink of an eye—
Mommy came home with another baby, little Rolee
Polee. Curlee Girlee wasn't the youngest anymore.

And there was something else. She wasn't the only one with curly hair!

She couldn't wait to tell her bouncy, roly-poly baby sister how very lucky she was to have perfect curly-whirly hair!